VENTURES
AT
HOUND HOTEL

raintree
a Capstone company — publishers for children

Raintree is an imprint of Capstone Global Library Limited, a company incorporated in
England and Wales having its registered office at 264 Banbury Road, Oxford, OX2 7DY –
Registered company number: 6695582

www.raintree.co.uk
myorders@raintree.co.uk

Edited by Jill Kalz
Designed by Heidi Thompson
Original illustrations © Capstone Global Library Limited 2017
Illustrated by Deborah Melmon
Production by Tori Abraham
Originated by Capstone Global Library
Printed and bound in China.

ISBN 978-1-4747-2061-8 (paperback)
20 19 18 17 16
10 9 8 7 6 5 4 3 2 1

British Library Cataloguing in Publication Data
A full catalogue record for this book is available from the British Library.

Mighty Murphy

by Shelley Swanson Sateren

illustrated by Deborah Melmon

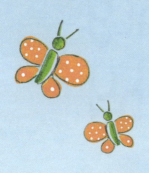

CONTENTS

CHAPTER 1
Tug of toothpaste................................... 9

CHAPTER 2
Watch the boy of iron............................ 16

CHAPTER 3
Alfie the Unstrong.................................. 24

CHAPTER 4
Envy stew... 30

CHAPTER 5
Cheesecake or cheeseburger?.............. 36

CHAPTER 6
Welcome back, big guy........................ 42

CHAPTER 7
A bite of cheesecake............................ 50

CHAPTER 8
New best friends.................................. 56

ADVENTURES
AT
HOUND HOTEL

IT'S TIME FOR YOUR ADVENTURE AT HOUND HOTEL!

At Hound Hotel, dogs are given the royal treatment. We are a top-notch boarding kennel. When your dog stays with us, we will follow your feeding schedule, take them for walks and tuck them into bed at night.

We are always just a short walk away from the dogs — the kennels are located in a heated building at the end of our driveway. Every dog has his or her own kennel, with a bed, blanket and water bowl.

Rest assured . . . a stay at the Hound Hotel is like a holiday for your dog. We have a large paddock, plenty of toys and a pool for the dogs to play in, in the summer. Your dog will love playing with the other guests.

HOUND HOTEL
WHO'S WHO

WINIFRED WOLFE

Hound Hotel is run by Winifred Wolfe, a lifelong dog lover. Winifred loves all types of dogs. She likes to get to know every breed. When she's not taking care of the canines, she writes books about — that's right — dogs.

ALFIE AND ALFREEDA WOLFE

Winifred's young twins help out as much as they can. Whether your dog needs gentle attention or extra playtime, Alfreeda and Alfie provide special services you can't find anywhere else. Your dog will never get bored whilst these two are helping out.

WOLFGANG WOLFE

Winifred's husband helps out at the hotel whenever he can, but he spends much of his time travelling to study packs of wolves. Wolfgang is a real wolf lover — he even named his children after pack leaders, the alpha wolves. Every wolf pack has two alpha wolves: a male wolf and a female wolf, just like the Wolfe family twins.

Next time your family goes on holiday, bring your dog to Hound Hotel.

Your pooch is sure to have a howling good time!

CHAPTER 1

Tug of toothpaste

I'm Alfie Wolfe, and there's one thing I hate: the fact that my twin sister, Alfreeda, is stronger than I am.

There, I said it. Out loud. For the whole world to hear.

But this story isn't about how much I stink in the Strength Department. Well, not totally. It's about a powerful dog called Murphy. A Rottweiler, to be exact. A Rottweiler that weighed about 45 kilograms, to be exacter.

Forty-five kilograms of pure muscle (and fur and bones, of course), to be exactest.

The adventure started early one morning last month. Much too early. My dog-shaped alarm clock barked at seven, for Pete's sake. TOO EARLY.

I banged the buttons on top until the clock shut up.

"Did you *have* to wake me up this early?" I asked it with a groan.

As usual, the clock-dog just stared at me.

Suddenly I remembered and sat up fast. A Rottweiler was coming to Hound Hotel that morning. Murphy the Rottie. Murphy the Dog of Iron!

Murphy was, paws down, the strongest visitor who had ever stayed at our dog hotel.

After he'd stayed here last summer, Mum had said, "Never again!" But Murphy's owner had a wedding to go to, and Murphy couldn't go along. Every other kennel had said no. So Mum gave in and said she'd take Murphy, for just one night. She can be a softie sometimes.

I couldn't wait to see that beefy guy again! Shame my dad couldn't see Murphy. Dad likes big dogs best. But he was in Canada again, studying wolf packs. That's his job.

I leapt out of bed. I had to beat Alfreeda to breakfast and call dibs on Murphy. I just *had* to spend time with him first.

I yanked off my pyjamas and dug through some piles of dirty clothes. I found a pair of dirty jeans and a stained Hound Hotel T-shirt. I got dressed and bolted to the bathroom.

Oh no, I thought. Alfreeda was standing by the sink, all ready for the workday. She wore jeans and a Hound Hotel T-shirt too – except hers were fresh smelling and clean.

And, of course, her face was washed. And her poodle-like hair was brushed. (I've got the same kind of hair, and I'm telling you, brushing it is *not* a piece of cake.)

Alfreeda reached for the toothpaste.

"Hey, give me that," I said, jumping towards the tube.

"No way, Alfie," she said. "I got here first."

We both dived at the toothpaste. She got a tight hold on one end. I got the other.

She tugged her end. I tugged mine.

"Give it *back*, Alfie," she snapped.

"Nope," I said.

"Yes!"

She yanked harder. So did I. Then she pulled with alpha-kid strength and yanked the tube right out of my hand.

"Ow!" I said.

My fingers actually burned. I rubbed them. But rubbing didn't help. So I ran cold water over them. That didn't help either. How a person can get burned by a plastic tube of toothpaste is a mystery to me. But I did.

Alfreeda grinned and put toothpaste onto her toothbrush. She screwed the cap back on and then handed me the tube.

"I call Murphy," I said, even though I knew Mum would make that decision.

"Ha," Alfreeda said through a mouthful of foam. "Tell me another good joke."

"You heard me," I said. "I called him first."

Alfreeda spat in the sink. In her I'm-SO-tired-of-explaining-things-to-my-stupid-brother voice, she said, "When will you ever listen to Mum's rules, Alfie? The first child who's *totally* ready for the workday gets to pick a favourite dog to play with. I'm ready F-I-R-S-T. So *I'll* get Murphy today. Step aside."

I didn't move.

We had a shoving match in the middle of the bathroom.

I won't say who ran out of the door first, except that I was left standing there, holding the stupid toothpaste.

I tried to unscrew the cap. I couldn't.

"Aargh!" I yelled, throwing the tube into the bath.

Then I tore downstairs. I was *not* going to let Alfreeda hog that cool dog all day!

CHAPTER 2
Watch the boy of iron

I won't say who got to the kitchen first.
But the winner stole the only free chair at the
kitchen table.

"There's nowhere for me to sit," I said.

The other chairs were piled with Mum's
writing stuff – books, papers, pens, lots of
coffee cups. She had another book deadline
breathing down her neck. (When she wasn't

caring for dogs in real life, she wrote stories about them.)

Mum stared at her computer screen until finally noticing I was chairless.

"Come here, Alfie," she said, clearing a chair and patting the seat.

I sat and grabbed a piece of buttered toast.

And that's when I got a great idea: I'd butter her up! I didn't waste a second. I tipped my head sideways and smiled, sweet as cheesecake. "You look very pretty this morning, Mother dear."

Mum stared at me. Her hair stuck out in ten directions. Her eyes were red and tired-looking. Dark circles ringed them too. Honestly, she looked like a raccoon that needed a long holiday. And a hairbrush.

"What do you want, Alfie?" she asked.

"Can I play with Murphy first, *please?*"
I begged. "Alfreeda hogged Herbie all day
yesterday. It's my turn to pick a favourite dog."

Herbie was a teensy Yorkshire terrier.
He stayed at our hotel a lot.

Alfreeda rolled her eyes. "You didn't finish
your chores yesterday, Alfie. *I* did, of course.
That's why I got Herbie all to myself. I'll beat
you at chores today too. So *I* get to play with
Murphy in the paddock first."

Mum shook her head. "Sorry," she said.
"Neither of you is going to play with Mighty
Murphy today."

Alfreeda choked on her juice. "What?"

"How come?" I asked.

"Remember when Murphy fence-fought
with Cheesecake last summer?" Mum asked.

"Yeah," I said. (Cheesecake is a cow from the farm next door.) "He kept sticking his nose through holes in the chain-link fence, trying to bite Cheesecake."

"That gave him a cut on his nose," Alfreeda said. "He almost broke the fence down too."

"That's right," Mum said. "I hate to think what Murphy would've done to poor Cheesecake if he'd reached her. That's why I said he could never stay here again. But his owner begged me. So I finally said Murphy could come for one night. On one condition."

"What's the condition?" I asked.

"That he stay in his pen the whole time," Mum said. "Except for short breaks."

"What?" Alfreeda cried. "He can only go outside for a couple of minutes?"

"Yes," Mum said. "And he must be on a lead."

"He'll be so bored," I said.

"Yeah," Alfreeda said. "Come on, Mum. Let me take him on walks around the paddock. I'll keep him on a lead and on the east side, away from Cheesecake."

"Sorry, Alfreeda," Mum said, shaking her head. "You're not strong enough to handle that powerful dog."

"That's right," I said. "But *I* am."

Alfreeda burst out laughing. "Murphy would pull you flat on your face in a second."

"He would not," I said.

"He would," she said.

"Would totally not. And I'll prove it. I'll show you how strong I am. Watch this."

I jumped off my chair and dragged it across the kitchen. I set it in the doorway between the kitchen and the living room. Then I stood on the chair and reached up high.

"I've practised this in my room a couple of times," I said. "Watch the boy of iron."

Alfreeda covered her mouth with her hands. She started to make choking noises.

I stood on my toes and straightened my back. I reached up even higher. Finally, just barely, I touched the top of the door frame. (We've got tall doors in our big old farmhouse.)

I held tight with my fingertips – my left hand on the living room side, my right hand on the kitchen side. Then I pulled myself up.

My feet lifted off the chair, and my head touched the top of the door frame.

"See?" I said. "A pull-up! Yes, sir, that's how strong I've got. Look how many I can do."

Alfreeda slowly dropped her hands from her mouth.

"That's right, sis," I said. "Watch the master, and learn the true meaning of strength."

Right in a row, I did *three* pull-ups. BAM! BAM! BAM!

"Woo-hoo!" I cried. "If anyone around here can handle a full-grown Rottie, it's Alfie the Strong! Alfie the Alpha Guy!"

Alfreeda rolled her eyes. She hopped off her chair and marched over. "Move," she ordered. "Let me try."

"No. I'm not finished," I said.

I tried to do a fourth pull-up, but my arms started to shake like mad. I dropped and totally missed the chair. I landed on the floor, right on my rear end.

Alfreeda leapt over me as if I were a Yorkshire terrier. She jumped onto the chair and reached for the top of the door frame.

"Watch this, everyone," she said with a grin.

I couldn't believe what my sister did next.

CHAPTER 3

Alfie the Unstrong

Alfreeda did *nine* pull-ups in a row. NINE! One right after the other. Super fast. The top of her head touched the top of the door frame every time.

She almost made it to ten, but her arms started to shake. She dropped to the floor, all graceful-like. Like a cat. She grinned and took a bow.

"That was fun," she said. "I never knew I could do those. I'll have to practise in my room tonight. By bedtime I'll be able to do 25."

Mum patted my shoulder. Pity only made it worse. I was so upset, I couldn't even speak.

"For Pete's sake, you two," Mum said. "Always trying to be Number One in our pack. Just like dogs and wolves. I wish you'd stop it. You're both Number One in your own ways."

"Not helping, Mum," I mumbled.

"Alfreeda? Please go and check on Herbie. I fed him already this morning, but he could do with a walk. Take this with you."

Mum handed Alfreeda a walkie-talkie. Alfreeda clipped it to her jeans pocket and bolted out the door.

Mum sat me down at the kitchen table and patted my shoulder again. "Oh, Alfie," she said.

"I know you feel like a beta wolf around your sister sometimes."

"Sometimes?" I cried. "How about *all* the time? I always come in second next to her, in everything. That's me, Alfie the Underdog!"

I went on in a squeaky voice, "It's because she was born five minutes before me, isn't it? Well, it's not fair that she's always the best. The worst part right now is that she's STRONGER than me. It's not right!"

Just then Alfreeda's voice blasted into the kitchen. Mum took a walkie-talkie off the charger and held it near her ear.

"Mum?" Alfreeda's voice crackled. "I'm with Herbie by the apple trees. Brianne's van is pulling into the driveway. Over."

Brianne was the lady who brought dog food to our kennels.

"Thanks, Alfreeda," Mum said into her walkie-talkie. "I'll send Alfie out. Over."

Mum turned to me. "Alfie," she said, "please tell Brianne that I'm painting the storeroom this week. Tell her to leave the dog-food bags in the office."

"Okay," I said, sighing. Then I dragged my dumb beta self out to the driveway.

"Hey, Alfie, my man!" Brianne called. She punched my shoulder, friendly-like.

I almost fell over.

Here's the thing: Brianne is the tallest, strongest woman I've ever met, even stronger than my mum. Big muscles cover Brianne's arms as though she lifts heavy metal weights every day of her life.

"Hi, Brianne. Want some help?" I asked.

Why those words came out of my mouth, I don't know. I'd never carried one of those huge food bags before.

"Sure, Alfie," Brianne said grinning. "You get one bag. I'll get the other. Your mum only ordered two this week."

She lifted a gigantic bag from the back of her van. She tossed it onto the driveway as if it were a feather.

"That one's yours," she said.

"Uh, okay," I said.

Brianne lifted the other huge bag and laid it over her shoulder. It was as if she had lifted teensy Herbie, the Yorkie.

"Mum wants them in the office," I said. "She's painting the storeroom."

Brianne marched inside the front door as if she had nothing on her shoulder but air.

If Alfreeda gets to be that powerful one day, I'll NEVER measure up around here! Everyone will call me Alfie the Unstrong for the rest of my life. And I'll never, ever get to take a cool Rottweiler on walks.

I leaned over and tried to pull the bag up the driveway.

And what happened next . . . well, I don't think I can be honest about it.

CHAPTER 4
Envy Stew

Okay, I'll be honest.

I couldn't get that super-heavy dog-food bag to budge. Not one centimetre.

Suddenly little Herbie jumped onto the bag. He grinned at me and licked my face.

"Hi, Herb Old Boy," I said, patting his cute furry head.

My sister was standing right next to me, shaking her head.

"Hey, Herbie," she said, snapping her fingers. "Stay right there, on top of that bag. I'll give you a ride. Won't that be *fun*?"

Herbie yipped and plopped his little rear end right down.

Alfreeda leaned over and took hold of the bag with both hands. Then she dragged it the whole way down the long driveway, all the way to the kennel building. I'm. Not. Kidding.

I followed her. My feet got heavier and heavier as I walked. So did my beta heart.

Alfreeda tugged the bag up the sloped path to the office door. She pulled it across the office floor and all the way down the hall to the kennel room. (That's the big room at the back of the building where all of the dog pens are.)

She didn't even breathe hard or break a sweat.

She tugged that gigantic bag all the way to Herbie's pen. She stopped in front of the gate and said, "Alfreeda's taxi service. Free of charge for cute doggies."

Herbie wagged his tail as if he'd just been on the best ride in the world.

Alfreeda picked him up and carried him inside his pen. She latched the gate behind them. "I'll brush you now, okay?" she said. "Then we'll play catch."

Herbie yipped and wagged his tail.

I just stood there, staring at that big bag of dog food. I barely heard Brianne's van roar away. But I certainly heard (and felt) the Envy Stew bubbling in my stomach.

That's it, I thought. *I'm not going to be Alfie the Unstrong for the rest of my life. I'm going*

to do something about it. I'm going to become a
POWERHOUSE. As powerful as a Rottweiler.
Starting today!

I marched across the kennel room, past all
the junk in the way. See, all the stuff from the

storeroom had been moved in there — boxes, dog beds, even the heavy metal shelves — so Mum could paint the storeroom walls.

Finally I found what I needed: a small, sturdy table on wheels. I wheeled it to the centre of the room and climbed on top of it.

"*What* are you doing, Alfie?" Alfreeda rolled her eyes. (I wished they'd roll out of her head and right out of the back door.)

I didn't answer.

A strong pipe ran the whole length of the kennel room, near the ceiling. I reached up and took hold of it with both hands. I'd practise pull-ups on that pipe all morning, until I could do 26 in a row. Alfreeda wouldn't be able to do 25 until bedtime.

Ha, I thought. *Pretty soon I'll be able to beat her. Then I'll get to take Murphy for a walk.*

I breathed in deep and gathered all the strength in my skinny beta arms. I got busy becoming Alfie the Strong. Alfie the Master of a Full-Grown Rottie.

I'd be quick about it too.

CHAPTER 5

Cheesecake or cheeseburger?

I did one alpha-kid pull-up from the ceiling pipe super fast.

Then another. And another.

But in the middle of the fourth pull-up, my arms turned as soft as tinned dog food.

I frowned at Alfreeda. "Would you *please* stop laughing?" I snapped. "I'm trying to practise here."

"Sorry," she squeaked.

She didn't sound very sorry.

I tried again, but I couldn't finish pull-up number four.

It was then that Mum's voice crackled over the walkie-talkie.

"Alfreeda?" she said. "Murphy's owner has just driven. I'll be right down to get Murphy into his kennel. Make sure Herbie is in his pen. You know how scared he gets around big dogs. And he's never been around one as large as Mighty Murphy. Over."

"I've already got Herbie in his pen, Mum," Alfreeda replied. "With the gate latched. Over."

"Great," Mum said. "Murphy and I will be there in a minute. Over."

I tried AGAIN to do a fourth pull-up.

Impossible, I thought with a groan. *I've got the muscles of a Yorkshire terrier. Mum will never let me spend time with a Rottweiler. Ever.*

Suddenly some loud, deep barking surprised me. I lost my hold and dropped onto the table. The table wiggled, shook and rolled a little, but somehow I managed to keep my balance.

"Whoa, boy," Mum cried as Murphy yanked her into the kennel room. He headed straight for the door to the paddock. (The paddock is a grassy fenced-in area for the dogs. It's right behind the kennel building.)

"Why is he pulling so hard?" Mum cried. "I didn't have this much trouble holding his lead last summer!"

"I bet he remembers Cheesecake," I said. "He wants that cow. I bet he wants to turn Cheesecake into a cheeseburger and have her for a tasty morning snack."

"Alfie!" Mum said.

"Well, I bet it's true," I said.

Murphy gave an extra-hard yank on the leash. Mum shot forward and tripped over the dog-food bag Alfreeda had left on the floor.

"Aaah!" Mum cried. Her feet and legs flew behind her. She shot to the floor and landed, full force, on her right hand. "Ow!"

The instant she hit the floor, she let go
of the lead. Murphy ran straight towards the
closed door. He only made it a metre, though.
A hard yank stopped him in his tracks. He
clawed the floor and barked, but
he couldn't move forward any further.

Then I saw why. His lead had caught on
one of the storeroom shelves.

Actually it was a tall, wide metal tower
with *five* shelves in it, loaded with boxes.
Heavy boxes, full of soap bottles and stuff.

Murphy tugged harder on the lead, trying to
get to the door – and Cheesecake.

The tower started to tip. It squeaked and
groaned. Box after box slid off the shelves and
landed with a THUD! THUD! THUD!

"Stop, Murphy!" Mum cried. "Stop pulling!
Sit! Stay!"

Too late.

The shelves fell forwards – CRASH! – right
on top of Herbie's pen.

With Herbie and my sister inside.

CHAPTER 6

Welcome back, big guy

For a few seconds, the kennel room was as quiet as a dog playing dead.

"Alfreeda? Are you and Herbie okay in there?" Mum asked.

"I think so," Alfreeda said. "I saw the shelves coming, so I jumped back. I had Herbie in my arms. Nothing hit us. But Herbie's shivering like mad."

"Try to calm him down," Mum said. "Ms Frill will be here in ten minutes to pick him up."

Fussy Ms Frill was Herbie's owner. She called Herbie her baby.

"If Ms Frill thinks Herbie got hurt, she'll never bring him back here," I said.

"I know," Mum said. "Thank goodness the pen fence is strong."

The shelves were leaning against Herbie's pen. Mum reached under them and tried to open Herbie's gate.

"It won't open," she said.

"We're trapped in here?" Alfreeda cried.

"Calm down," Mum said, "or you'll upset Herbie more. We'll think of something."

Murphy sat still now, panting hard. I rubbed his neck. "Hey, big guy, welcome back."

He licked my hand.

Mum tried to lift the shelves off the pen. "Ow!" she cried and rubbed her wrist. "I think it's sprained from when I fell. Great. Now I'm one-handed, with a Rottie to care for and a trapped Yorkie to save."

I leapt off the table. "I'll help you, Mum," I said. "Come on. Use your good arm."

Together the two of us tried to lift the shelves. They didn't budge.

For once my sister wasn't laughing.

"Hurry!" she cried. "Do something! Ms Frill will be here soon!"

"I know! Calm down!" I said.

Hearing us shouting, Murphy jumped up and barked loudly at the door again. He tugged with all his might.

"Yes! Go, Murphy!" I said. "Pull the shelves off Herbie's pen. That's right. Keep going."

But not even Mighty Murphy could move those shelves. Then I noticed why: the shelves were caught on the gate latch.

"They have to be lifted from above," I said. "I've got an idea. I'll be right back."

I ran to the kennel kitchen and found a box of dog treats. In seconds I was back in the kennel room, dumping treats on the floor in front of Murphy.

"Here, boy," I said. "Feast on these."

Straight away he stopped tugging and started to gobble the treats.

Super fast I laid a trail of treats from Murphy's nose to his pen. Next I untangled the lead from the shelves.

The treat trail led Murphy into his kennel. I patted his head, ducked out and latched his pen gate behind me.

"Don't worry, Mum," I said, patting her arm. "I've got a plan. I'll be back in a minute."

I raced to the garage, found a long rope and raced back. I jumped on the little table and threw the rope over the ceiling pipe. Then I jumped off, moved the table next to the shelves, and climbed back on.

After that I tied one end of the rope to the top of the metal tower. I tied a good, strong knot, just like Dad had taught me.

Next I ran to the kitchen and found the last box of dog treats. It was only half full. *I hope it's enough*, I thought.

I dashed back to Murphy's pen and dumped the treats on the floor right in front of him.

He gobbled them up fast. I barely had enough time to tie the rope to his collar. I made the tightest double knot I could.

"Hurry, Alfie," Mum begged. "Ms Frill will be here in a couple of minutes."

Finally I ran to the window on the back wall. As soon as I opened it, Cheesecake's mooing filled the kennel room. *MOO! MOO!*

Murphy barked like crazy. He charged out of his pen, straight towards the open window. The rope got tight and tugged on the shelves.

The metal tower wiggled and shook.

Mum's eyes got huge.

"Come on, Murphy! Come on!" I called. "Come and see Cheesecake!"

Murphy barked his head off and yanked like a workhorse. He inched closer to the window. The shelves started to lift off Herbie's pen.

And that's when the doorbell rang.

"Oh, no," Mum cried. "Ms Frill is here!"

CHAPTER 7

A bite of cheesecake

Yip! Yip! Yip! That's what the kennel building's doorbell sounds like. You can hear it in every room.

It made Murphy bark even louder.

"I'll take care of Ms Frill," Mum said. "Alfreeda, bring Herbie to me the *second* the gate is unblocked. Don't come out until the shelves are safely upright."

"Okay, Mum," Alfreeda said.

I turned back to Murphy. "Come on, big guy! You've got to raise those shelves a bit more. Almost there. Where's Cheesecake, huh? Where is that cow?"

Murphy tugged but not hard enough. So I started to moo – right along with Cheesecake. *MOO! MOO! MOO! MOO!*

That did it.

Murphy barked like mad and pulled harder. All of his muscles shook. His claws left scratch marks on the floor too. I'd never seen a dog work so hard.

He yanked and barked and panted. And then, at last, the shelves stood upright again!

"Wow!" I cried. "You did it, Murphy! But stop pulling now, okay?"

"Yeah," Alfreeda said, "don't make the shelves fall the other way!" She ran out of Herbie's pen with Herbie in her arms.

But Murphy wouldn't stop pulling that rope.

I quickly wheeled the table beside the metal tower and jumped up on it. "That's enough! Stop pulling, Murphy!"

But did he listen? No. Of course not. That dog wanted a bite of Cheesecake.

Then the shelves started to tip in the other direction – straight towards ME.

My heart pounded. *Goodbye, sweet life*, I thought, swallowing hard. *I never knew it would all end so soon – skinny, weak little me getting squashed by a load of big, heavy metal shelves.*

No – wait – I don't want it to end this way! It can't end this way!

I started to imagine that I, Alfie Wolfgang Wolfe, was a powerhouse Rottweiler. I took a deep breath and pushed against that big metal tower. Somehow I found strength in my arms that I never knew I had.

I kept pushing until the shelves stood upright again. Then I drummed up all the strength in my ten fingers and pulled the strong knot apart. The rope fell to the floor.

Mum and Alfreeda rushed into the kennel room. That same second Murphy jumped at the wall and started to climb out of the window.

"Stop him!" Mum cried. "Grab the rope!"

I leapt off the table and dived for the rope. Alfreeda dived for it too.

Together we tugged with all our might. Murphy dug his claws into the floor and pulled in the other direction.

We pulled harder.

He didn't.

Without warning he lay down and played dead!

"Fine," I said. "Well, guess what? You're not too heavy for US, big guy."

"Nope," Alfreeda said. "Let's go, Alfie"

My sister and I dug in our heels and slid Murphy all the way across the room and into his pen. We patted his head, ducked out and latched the gate behind us.

We just stood there for about a minute, panting like a couple of pugs on a hot day.

Mum stared at us. "I cannot *believe* you two pulled that huge, heavy dog all that way," she said.

Alfreeda and I grinned and high-fived.

"So, Mum," I said. "Maybe Alfreeda and I could both hold Murphy's lead. Together we're as strong as you are. Can we take him outside together for short breaks? I mean, since you've only got one good arm right now."

Mum chewed her lip.

"Can we, Mum? Please?" Alfreeda begged.

CHAPTER 8

New best friends

"Okay," she said, nodding. "But if Murphy starts to fence-fight with Cheesecake, bring him straight back inside. I don't want anyone to get hurt. Or the fence to get destroyed."

"Got it," Alfreeda and I said at the same time.

I spun around to face Murphy, "Hey, Murphy. You've been here a while now. Do you need to go to the toilet?"

Murphy jumped up and barked. Alfreeda clipped his lead to his collar. Then both she and I got a strong hold on the lead.

"Come on, boy," Alfreeda said.

We led him out of his pen. As soon as we got through the gate, he darted right around us. He started to tug towards the paddock door.

I looked over my shoulder. Mum had her back turned to us. She was busy digging in the first-aid drawer.

I let go of the lead for a split second, just long enough to throw open the door. Then Murphy yanked us outside — so hard we almost fell flat on our faces. I kicked the door shut behind us.

"Murphy had better be quiet," Alfreeda said.

"I don't want Mum to hear."

"Yeah," I said. "We need to make his time outside last."

Suddenly Murphy started to bark like a fierce guard dog. He pulled us towards the fence, hard and fast. We kept tripping over our feet.

At the fence he stood on his back legs and clawed at the metal links.

"Stop!" Alfreeda cried. "You'll hurt yourself!"

Murphy kept barking and clawing the fence.

Cheesecake didn't seem to care. She stood in the middle of the meadow and stared at Murphy. She mooed a friendly moo.

"What's the problem, Murphy?" I shouted over his mad barking. "Is it because Cheesecake is bigger than you? Stronger than you? Well, that's no reason to get all mad. She's not going to hurt you, or us, or anyone. You DON'T have to protect my sister or me, Murphy!"

I don't think he heard a word I said.

"LOOK, you do NOT have to protect us, okay?" I yelled. "You're NOT in charge here, Murphy! WE are!"

That's when I had an idea.

Somehow I managed to unclip the lead from his collar. Then I scaled the fence and leapt to the other side. I walked over to Cheesecake and patted her warm, soft stomach. "Hey, Cheesecake Old Girl," I said. "Follow me."

I clipped the lead to her collar and then led her to the paddock fence. She followed, calm as a sleepy puppy.

Straight away Murphy stopped barking. He sat down and stared at us.

Nice and slowly I walked Cheesecake back and forth in front of the fence, just centimetres away from Murphy's nose. He didn't move a muscle. Only his eyeballs moved, left to right, right to left. He watched us parade back and forth.

"Wow," Alfreeda whispered.

"Yep," I said. "Now he knows who's Alpha Guy here." I pointed at myself and grinned.

Alfreeda nodded. "I remember something Mum told me last summer. A Rottie should never be allowed to think it's the alpha dog. It'll fight people or other animals for the leader role."

"Yep," I said. "That's what I thought."

"Cool," Alfreeda said. "Now Murphy knows that Cheesecake is an underdog too. So he doesn't have to fight her. Way to go, Alf."

"Thanks." I took a bow.

Suddenly Murphy stuck his nose through one of the fence links.

"Murphy, don't!" Alfreeda ordered him.

Cheesecake pulled on the lead and leaned towards Murphy. In a blink she licked him, right on the nose.

Murphy froze. He didn't move a muscle.

I held my breath. Alfreeda's eyes opened super wide.

Murphy's little stump of a tail started to wag, and then . . . he licked Cheesecake. Right on her big pink nose.

After that my sister and I had a whole *new* problem. Murphy and Cheesecake wouldn't stop licking each other's faces.

"Isn't that just so cute and SWEET?" Mum called from the door.

"Whatever," I sighed.

"It's *not* great," Alfreeda said, rolling her eyes. "It's boring. We wanted to play with Murphy. Not watch him lick a cow's nose."

"Want to play catch?" I asked my sister.

"Okay," she said. "There's nothing better to do."

I dug in the box of dog toys and found a

ball. I darted to the east side of the paddock. Alfreeda stayed on the west.

"Ready?" I called. I wound up my arm to throw.

She nodded.

I threw the ball.

"Ow!" she yelled, catching the ball. She dropped it and blew on her hands. "That burned. Do you *have* to throw it so hard?"

"Uh, sorry," I said.

She tossed the ball back to me. I threw it again, softer this time.

I guess I didn't have to prove my strength anymore. I had already done that. Yes, maybe I was bad at pull-ups. But I could tie strong knots. I could push a heavy metal tower upright. I could help drag a full-grown Rottie across a floor. And I could burn my sister's hand with a power throw.

"Hey," I said. "Let's paint the storeroom together. Mum can't even open a tin of paint with just one hand."

"I call dibs on the ladder," she said. "I want to paint the high areas."

"*I* do!" I raced towards the door.

We had a shoving match in the doorway. I won't say who won, because I don't like to brag. But pretty soon, I got bored painting the high areas – right about the same time Murphy got bored with getting his face licked by Cheesecake.

So we two strong boys played catch the rest of the afternoon.

It was a perfect Hound Hotel day after all. Perfect with a capital P.

Is a Rottweiler the dog for you?

Hi! It's me, Alfreeda!

I bet you want your own big, strong Rottweiler now too, right? Of course you do! But actually, Rotties make good pets only for some families. Before you zoom off to buy or adopt one, here are some REALLY important facts you should know:

Rotties can hurt other pets, children or old people by mistake. They're super heavy and powerful and often don't know their own strength. Rottie puppies need special training if they're going to live with cats, other dogs, children or old people. Families should NOT adopt a full-grown Rottie unless they know for certain that it will accept children and pets it hasn't grown up with.

A Rottie must never think it's the leader in a family. If it does it will be too protective. That puts neighbours, visitors, postal workers, or other people's pets in real danger. Rotties need firm, strong adult leaders who know how to train them properly. But even the children in a family have to be trained to act like leaders around their Rottie. If your family can't or won't learn about proper Rottie training, do NOT get a Rottie. Get a goldfish instead.

Rotties must have a dog-proof, fenced garden in which to run. They need LOTS of exercise. Even if you have a fenced-in garden, the grown-ups in your family needs to take your Rottie for a long walk every day. If your family can't promise to do that, don't get a Rottie. Or any dog. Get a pet rock instead.

Okay, signing off for now . . . until the next adventure at Hound Hotel!

Yours very factually,

Alfreeda Wolfe

Glossary

alpha a person or animal who is the leader and is the best or most powerful one in a group

beta second in command

ceiling the upper surface inside a room

collar a thin band of leather or other material that a pet wears around its neck; often it has information that says who the animal belongs to in case it gets lost

envy wishing you could have something that someone else has or do something that he/she has done

fierce likely to attack or cause harm

boarding kennels a place where dogs are kept and cared for while their owners are away

latch a lock on a door or gate

manage to be able to do something that is hard

muscle a body part that produces movement

paddock smell fenced-in field where animals can exercise

pity a feeling of sadness for someone's troubles

protect to keep someone or something safe from harm

sprain to hurt a part of the body by twisting it too far or hard

Talk about it

1. Alfie is envious of his sister's strength at the beginning of the story. At first he feels sorry for himself. He puts himself down. But then he decides to get stronger by practising pull-ups. Think about a time that you were envious of someone. What did you do about your envy? How did you act? Could you have acted better? If so, how?

2. Explain, step by step, how Alfie showed Murphy that *he* (not Murphy) was the "alpha dog" at Hound Hotel.

Write about it

1. If Mighty Murphy could talk, how do you think he would describe the adventure he had at Hound Hotel? Write a paragraph from Murphy's point of view.

2. Write a letter to your parents that explains why you think a Rottweiler would, or would not, be a good dog for your family.

3. Write a one-page essay on Rottweilers. Use at least three sources.

About the author

Shelley Swanson Sateren grew up with five pet dogs: a beagle, a terrier mix, a terrier-poodle mix, a Weimaraner and a German shorthaired pointer. As an adult, she adopted a lively West Highland white terrier called Max. As well as having written many children's books, Shelley has worked as a children's book editor and in a children's bookshop. She lives in Minnesota, USA, with her husband, and has two grown-up sons.

About the illustrator

Deborah Melmon has worked as an illustrator for more than 25 years. After graduating from Academy of Art University in San Francisco, USA, she started her career illustrating covers for a weekly magazine supplement. Since then, she has produced artwork for more than 20 children's books. Her artwork can also be found on wrapping paper, greetings cards and fabric. Deborah lives in California, USA, and shares her studio with an energetic Airedale Terrier called Mack.

ADVENTURES AT HOUND HOTEL

Cool Crosby

Brothers and sisters can be the best. But they can also be the worst! Alfreeda is a giant pain in her twin brother's side, and Alfie can't stand her anymore. He's about to go crazy! Luckily, a laid-back German shepherd named Crosby (along with his pesky puppy brother) is checking into Hound Hotel. It's time for Alfie to learn how to keep his cool – dog style!

Drooling Dudley

Alfie Wolfe hates to clean. Cleaning is a waste of time! He likes being messy. He likes leaving his stuff all over the place. But Alfie is about to meet his messy match. Checking in at Hound Hotel today is a drool-filled English bulldog named Dudley. Thanks to this lovable lump, Alfie will see how quickly a little slobber can turn into big, big trouble!

Fearless Freddie

It's a dark and stormy day at Hound Hotel, and twins Alfie and Alfreeda are both feeling a little bit nervous. Even worse, every crash of thunder terrifies their newest guest, Freddie the beagle, who howls with fear. Not only are his howls upsetting, but he's scaring the other dogs! Which twin is brave enough to calm Freddie down?

Growling Gracie

Hound Hotel is packed! Alfie and Alfreeda and their mum are working day and night just to keep up. When Uncle Robert turns up with Twinkles, a champion Frisbee dog, Alfie spots an opportunity for some much needed fun. But Twinkles' "sister" Gracie, the grumpy golden retriever, has other plans. She doesn't want anyone near her pack, and she'll stop at nothing to keep Alfie away!

Homesick Herbie

Alfie and Alfreeda are looking forward to welcoming Herbie, a cute little Yorkshire terrier. But Herbie is not excited about being at Hound Hotel. The little puppy is so homesick that all he does is cry. Alfie's convinced that Herbie just needs some proper "boy" time, but Alfreeda insists on babying the dog instead. What does poor Herbie need to make Hound Hotel feel more like home?

Mighty Murphy

Hound Hotel never had a stronger guest than Murphy. The last time he visited, he was quite a handful for Alfie, Alfreeda, and their mum. He even got into a little trouble with the neighbor's cow, Cheesecake. Now the mighty Rottweiler is back. It'll take muscle and a lot of quick thinking to keep things under control– and to keep Murphy away from that cow!

Mudball Molly

Molly, a West Highland terrier, is supposed to be the flower girl for her owner's wedding. The mucky-pup hates being groomed, so Alfie is a back-up page boy. Alfie will do nearly anything to get out of the wedding, and his sister Alfreeda will go to any lengths to be included. But none of this matters when Molly loses the wedding rings in the doggie playground! Which of the twins will save the day and find the missing rings?

Stinky Stanley

Alfie and Alfreeda's mum is super proud of Hound Hotel. It's known for being clean and smelling fresh. But today something smells horrible – Alfie's feet! Picky Ms. Snoot is arriving soon, and she won't leave her Labrador retriever, Stanley, in a stinky hotel. It's a race to clean up, and in the end, Alfie may not be the only one who smells fishy!

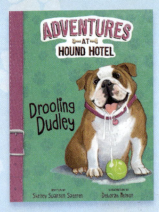

ADVENTURES AT **HOUND HOTEL**

Cool Crosby

WRITTEN BY Shelley Swanson Sateren   ILLUSTRATION BY Deborah Melmon

ADVENTURES AT **HOUND HOTEL**

Drooling Dudley

WRITTEN BY Shelley Swanson Sateren   ILLUSTRATION BY Deborah Melmon

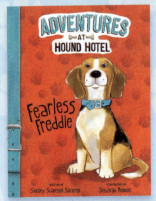

ADVENTURES AT **HOUND HOTEL**

Fearless Freddie

WRITTEN BY Shelley Swanson Sateren   ILLUSTRATION BY Deborah Melmon

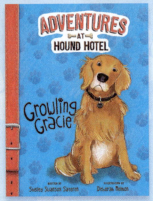

ADVENTURES AT **HOUND HOTEL**

Growling Gracie

WRITTEN BY Shelley Swanson Sateren   ILLUSTRATION BY Deborah Melmon

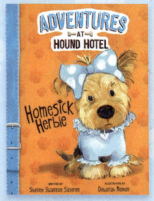

ADVENTURES AT **HOUND HOTEL**

Homesick Herbie

WRITTEN BY Shelley Swanson Sateren   ILLUSTRATION BY Deborah Melmon

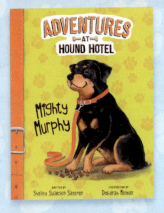

ADVENTURES AT **HOUND HOTEL**

Mighty Murphy

WRITTEN BY Shelley Swanson Sateren   ILLUSTRATION BY Deborah Melmon

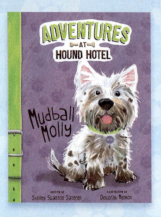

ADVENTURES AT **HOUND HOTEL**

Mudball Molly

WRITTEN BY Shelley Swanson Sateren   ILLUSTRATION BY Deborah Melmon

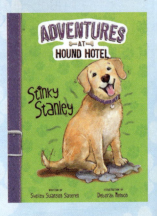

ADVENTURES AT **HOUND HOTEL**

Stinky Stanley

WRITTEN BY Shelley Swanson Sateren   ILLUSTRATION BY Deborah Melmon

www.raintree.co.uk